HUESLANDIA:
At Another Time . . . At Another Place

Written by: Michael Murphy

Illustrated by: Carissa McDonald

MURLOR BOOKS

Kindle Direct Publishing

Dedicated to my Mother-Katherine—who taught us that everyone deserves our respect.

FOREWARD

At another time . . . . and in another place:

"He has endeavored to prevent the population of these states; for that purpose obstructing the Laws for Naturalization of Foreigners; refusing to pass others to encourage their migrations hither ...

In Congress Assembled
July 4, 1776
The Declaration of Independence

Hueslandia

At another time … and in another place:

There once was a country called

Hueslandia. The people of Hueslandia were

of many different **hues**. They were red and

blue, purple and green, pink and yellow,

white and black, brown and tan and all the

hues in between!!

But it had not always been that way.

Hueslandia had a long and varied

history. The original Hueslandians had

lived there for thousands of years. They had

developed many different cultures,

languages, and religions. They mostly lived

off the land and in harmony with nature. But

often they did not live in harmony with each

other. That would pose a problem in their

future.

Soon they were not alone. Immigrants began to arrive in Hueslandia. They came from a long distance over a vast ocean. They came from places with odd names like Britlandia and Franclandia and Gerlandia. They spoke new languages and followed different religions. Many came to Hueslandia for **freedom**. They wanted to practice their religion as they wished. Others sought land and economic freedom. Some came to escape civil war and **persecution**. Others came so they might have a say in how they were ruled.

At first these new Hueslandians sought to live alongside the native Hueslandians. But then their attitude changed. Slowly they began to push the natives farther into the vast interior of Hueslandia. Because these natives did not always live peacefully with each other, they were not able to organize and resist the newcomers. It would be a long time before the native Hueslandians would enjoy the same freedoms as these new arrivals.

The new Hueslandians were ruled by a king that lived thousands of miles across the vast ocean from Hueslandia. Because of this great distance, the Hueslandians began to make their own rules and laws. In effect, they began to govern themselves.

The king did not like this and attempted to assert his power. He imposed many laws regulating the Hueslandians' activities. Most importantly he tried to tax the people of Hueslandia.

The Hueslandians put up with these rules and laws for many years, but finally they grew tired of the king's policies. A great rebellion broke out among the Hueslandians. The king decided to put the rebellion down and sent a great army to subject the Hueslandians to his rule. A long

and bitter war was fought by the

Hueslandians against the king's army.

Finally, the Hueslandians won their freedom

and their independence.

And that is where our story really

begins. You see when the Hueslandians set

up their new country they stated some

especially important principles for the

citizens of Hueslandia to follow. The most

important of these were that all

Hueslandians were created equal in the eyes

of the law. They also said that every

Hueslandian had certain rights that could not

be taken away from them. Life, liberty, and

the pursuit of happiness were among these

rights. They also set up a government by

which the Hueslandians could vote to

choose their leaders.

VOTE

HERE

The trouble was, however, that these
ideas were not always equally provided to
all Hueslandians. There always seemed to be
a struggle within the Hueslandians: A
struggle between hope and fear; between the
better angels of their nature and the dark

impulses of distrust and **discrimination**; between love and hate.

In fact, from the very beginning of their country some Hueslandians had been enslaved!! These Afrilandians, as they were known, had been stolen from their native lands and brought to Hueslandia on a long, **perilous**, and cruel sea voyage. Many had died on the way. When they arrived in Hueslandia, they were subjected to a **dehumanizing** auction where they were sold to the highest bidder.

Then they were transported to plantations where they were forced to work under intolerable conditions—beaten and whipped if they did not work hard enough or failed to satisfy their master.

Eventually some Hueslandians saw the evils of this system. They began to oppose the enslavement of people. Some of the slaves, at great risk to life and limb, escaped and began to speak out about the horrors of the system. Many more Hueslandians began to see slavery for what it was- a denial of all that Hueslandia was supposed to stand for. But those who favored it would not allow the system to end peacefully. And there it was—that first big challenge for the soul of the Hueslandians—the struggle between good or evil—the light or the darkness.

Then a Hueslandian was elected as leader who said Hueslandia could not remain half free and half slave.

Soon the Hueslandians began to argue

among themselves. The arguments grew

bitter and **divisive**. Then a terrible war

broke out—a terrible civil war –where

Hueslandians fought other Hueslandians.

The long and costly war lasted four long

years. When it was over, slavery was

abolished forever in Hueslandia. But sadly,

the leader who had called for slavery's end

had lost his life in the war. Even more

disheartening was that the former slaves,

who had won their freedom, soon faced

discrimination and legal limits on their

rights. That would set off a century long

struggle to secure those rights- a struggle

many Hueslandians continue to this day!

That was another challenge to the creed for

which Hueslandia was supposed to

represent: another struggle for the better

angels of their nature.

Even before this struggle over slavery

had begun, Hueslandia had become a nation

that was incredibly attractive to immigrants.

The chance to experience the freedoms and

economic opportunity enjoyed by many

Hueslandians was a strong **incentive** for many people searching for a better life— despite the hardships and possible discrimination that might be faced in coming to this new land. One of the first major groups to arrive in Hueslandia was the

FAMINE	POVERTY

Eirelandians.

The Eirelandians had experienced a terrible crop failure in their native land—a crop failure that happened several years in a row. As a result, millions of Eirelandians immigrated to Hueslandia. Once they had arrived, they faced discrimination for their religious beliefs and false impressions about their **work ethic**. In fact, when these new immigrants went to apply for jobs, they often found signs posted that said "No Eirelandians Need Apply."

Another time . . . Another place:

"Our attitude towards immigration reflects our faith in the American ideal. We have always believed it possible for men and women who start at the bottom to rise as far as their talent and energy allow. Neither race nor place of birth should affect their chances."

Robert F. Kennedy

The Hueslandians even formed secret

societies who worked to keep the

immigrants out of Hueslandia. One group

called itself the "Do Not Know Its." They

called themselves this because if ever they

were questioned about their anti-immigrant

beliefs they would reply "I do not know anything about it," to their **inquisitors.** They tried to get laws passed to restrict immigration and keep out the foreigners.

But over time the Eirelandians worked hard to overcome the discrimination and **stereotypes** they faced. Slowly they were accepted by the other Hueslandians. And this became a pattern in Hueslandia. People would arrive from distant lands and cultures. They would arrive with different beliefs and customs, different religions and languages, different experiences and ideas, different

talents and abilities. They too would face

discrimination and **ostracism**; sometimes

they even faced **racism**.

They too would work hard and

eventually overcome the obstacles they

faced. They would come to Hueslandia with

all these differences-face discrimination—

work hard—add their talents and ideas to the

culture of Hueslandia—often serve in

Hueslandia's armed forces when the nation

faced external threats or invasion from a

foreign power-overcome the discrimination—and gain acceptance and **assimilation**!! The pattern would be repeated again and again. Out of this process—which some called a "**melting pot**"—the immigrants became Hueslandians.

Another time …. Another place:
"We have become not a melting pot but a beautiful mosaic. Different people, different beliefs, different yearnings, different hopes, different dreams."
— Jimmy Carter

And one of the most important parts of this

process – and one sometimes overlooked—

was that the immigrants had something else

in common. All of them were drawn to

Hueslandia because it offered them

freedom!! Their adoptive home offered

them an opportunity to make a better life for themselves and their children. That commitment to the ideals of Hueslandia was part of the process that made these immigrants Hueslandians.

These immigrants came from all over. They came form southern and eastern Eurlandia; from Ruslandia, from Chilandsia and Jalandia. There were Ilandians and Polandians. Grelandians and Bullandians. Allandians and Chelandians.

They filled the farms and the factories of Hueslandia. They built the railroads and bridges. They were the meat packers, the tool and die makers, the machine operators, the maids and the seamstresses. The iron workers and steelmakers. The textile worker, the laborer, the farm hand, and the construction worker. Their hard work helped make Hueslandia an industrial power. They helped make Hueslandia's economy the envy of the world.

Then war came to Hueslandia in a far-
off distant place. Once again, a king had
tried to impose his will on other free people.
Hueslandians answered the call. Many were
the sons of the immigrants who had poured

into Hueslandia from these same distant

lands now under **siege**. Some were even the

immigrants themselves only having arrived

in Hueslandia a few years before the war.

They filled the ranks and became the

soldiers and the sailors who fought and won

this great war for Hueslandia and its **allies**.

When the war was over and the troops came home, many Hueslandians began to struggle once more with their "better angels." Fear of the many immigrants who had entered the country in the decades before the war began to grow. Some of those immigrants had spoken strange languages, followed different religions, and had unusual political beliefs. So, a move was made to stop the flow of immigrants into Hueslandia. A new law was passed that set up a **quota** system. It limited the number of immigrants who could enter Hueslandia. It also restricted the type of immigrant who could come into the nation. It favored the type of person who had come to Hueslandia in its colonial time. Back when that king had ruled over Hueslandia from that great distance.

And so, the quota system became the new reality in Hueslandia.

Life in Hueslandia went onward. A decade of **prosperity** was followed by a decade of economic collapse and depression. Then another war came along. Hueslandia once again joined its allies and help to defeat a **vile** and **vicious** dictator who had tried to rule the world. He had also murdered millions of innocent people.

Some Hueslandians were critical of

their government for not doing more to

help the innocents who were being

slaughtered to come to Hueslandia—

some had been turned away virtually

sitting at the doorstep of Hueslandia. But this was soon forgotten as Hueslandia emerged from this war as both an economic powerhouse and a world leader.

The years after the war also brought some of the problems of Hueslandia into the light. Since the end of slavery nearly 100 years earlier, the descendents of those slaves had faced hardship, discrimination, and racism. Now a new leader emerged in Hueslandia—a man who was not an elected leader—but a man of justice and vision.

He would lead a great social uprising, based

on peace, love, and **non-violence** that would

bring about new laws that would begin to

bring change to Hueslandia. Slowly, the

rights that had been denied minority citizens

of Hueslandia began to be restored. This

included the descendants of those Native

Hueslandians, who were the original

inhabitants of Hueslandia. The struggle

would continue, and continues to today, but

things began to change for the better.

Then another change happened. About

twenty years after the end of this war, a new

leader was elected in Hueslandia. He

wanted to end **poverty** and create a

"Magnificent Society." He accomplished a

great many things for the poor of

Hueslandia. As part of his plan, he changed immigration laws again.

The quotas remained, but the new rules favored immigrants from different places. Rules would also be set up for those who were fleeing from religious persecution, civil war, discrimination, gang violence, and bloodshed. These people could seek **asylum** in Hueslandia.

And so, a new wave of immigrants began to arrive in Hueslandia. There was one big difference in these new immigrants—many of them were of darker hues-browns and tans and blacks. Many of them came from some of the poorest parts of the world. But, like the earlier waves of immigrants, they came to Hueslandia seeking a better life for themselves and their families.

The new law had done one other thing, however. For the first time it had greatly limited the number of immigrants from the countries that bordered Hueslandia. Many of the people from these countries had entered

Hueslandia only temporarily. They had come to help harvest the vast fruit and vegetable crops grown in Hueslandia. Then, at the end of the harvest season, they had returned home.

However, the need for these workers did not end. So, a new problem emerged. Many people began to enter Hueslandia illegally. The need was great and many Hueslandians hired the illegals to work in the fields and on the farms, on construction crews, and as domestic workers. Many of the illegals stayed in Hueslandia. They became known as **undocumented** workers.

Some had even brought their young children with them to Hueslandia. These young children would grow up in Hueslandia. Hueslandia was their home. They wanted to become full-fledged citizens of their adopted home. One leader had started a program to provide them with protection and with hope for full citizenship. These young people became know as "Dreamers."

So, it came to pass that illegal immigration became a political issue in Hueslandia. Every few years-especially during elections-politicians would offer solutions to the issue. Some would talk about **amnesty** for the undocumented workers. Others would promote a "pathway to citizenship" for the illegals. Others would take a harsher view and call for arrest, detention, and **deportation** of these undocumented workers.

A debate also raged in Hueslandia about

the immigrants. Some thought the country

was big enough and rich enough to absorb

the immigrants. Those with this viewpoint

believed that immigrants were a part of

Hueslandia's story. They thought

immigrants brought renewal to Hueslandia

and added their skills, ideas, and talents to

the great melting pot that Hueslandia had

become. Others took a different view. They

saw the immigrants as "invaders." They

were afraid the immigrants would take over

Hueslandia. And there was no sense in

denying it—they were afraid of the hues of

these immigrants. That ugly feature of

Hueslandia's past-racism-reared its head

again.

The struggle among Hueslandians

between the better angels of their nature and

the forces of fear was renewed. Most

Hueslandians agreed that the nation needed

secure borders. They agreed that a safe and

sane immigration policy was not only

desirable, but in the best interests of both

Hueslandia and its people and the

immigrants trying to gain access to the

country. But reaching agreement on how to

achieve this goal was difficult.

And then it was time for an election!

One of the candidates for the election as

Hueslandia's leader started his campaign

with attacks on the immigrants coming to

Hueslandia. He called them names. He said

all they did when they arrived in Hueslandia

was commit crimes. He implied that they were going to overrun Hueslandia. None of that was true. Still, he appealed to fear. He appealed to racism. He appealed to the worst angels of the Hueslandians' nature.

The signature promise of his campaign was that he would build a barrier to keep the immigrants out of Hueslandia. He also promised that the Hueslandians would not have to pay for the barrier. Instead the countries that the immigrants came from would pay for his two-thousand-mile barrier.

Few people thought he would win the election. But he did.

As soon as he was sworn in, he began to take steps against the immigrants. He issued a ban against a certain religious group and would not allow them into Hueslandia. The children who had been brought to Hueslandia by the parents-the "Dreamers" saw the program that protected them come to an end. Suddenly they faced possible deportation from the only place they had known as home.

Then, worst of all, immigrants that arrived at Hueslandia's border were separated from their children. The children were put in cages. Some were shipped off to distant parts of Hueslandia. No plan was put in place to reunite them with their parents.

Some critics of this action discovered that

these parents and their children might never

be reunited!

Many Hueslandians disliked these new

policies and began to resist the new leader.

They organized protests. They published

news stories. They went to court to stop the

leader from carrying out many of his

programs. They had some success, but the

leader had a lot of power. He continued

with many of his actions despite the protests.

Then he tried to build his barrier.

He did not think much of the

immigrants' abilities. He thought them to be

inferior. He thought any kind of barrier

would stop them from entering Hueslandia.

What he also did not realize was that barriers seldom worked. Nearly every barrier built in history had failed. These artificial barricades had never achieved the goal their builders had envisioned. The Great Wall of Chinlandia had failed. The Berlandia Wall had failed. Hadrialania's Wall had failed.

But that did not stop this new leader. He was determined to build a wall.

So, at first, he tried a "Wall of Straw." But the "Wall of Straw" didn't work. The immigrants just tore it down or burned holes in the straw. But it really failed because there was an idea stronger than his straw.

Next, he tried a "**Formidable** Fence" of chain link. But it didn't work either. The immigrants and refugees just climbed over his formidable fence. It too failed because there was an idea stronger than his formidable fence.

Nothing seemed to work.

He was **persistent,** however. He tried again. (And, by the way, all these barriers were NOT being paid for by the immigrants' countries! They were being paid by the taxpayers of Hueslandia! A promise broken!)

This time he built a "Barrier of Barbed Wire." But, once again he failed. You see it was easy to cut through the wire. As with the other barriers, the "Barrier of Barbed Wire" was ineffective because there was an idea stronger than barbed wire.

Next, he tried a "Wooden Wall of

Wonder." But alas it too failed. The

immigrants just cut holes in the wood. But,

it failed because there was an idea

stronger than his wooden wall.

Now the leader was angry! He realized

he had underestimated the immigrants. (In

truth he had underestimated the idea!!)

So, the next time he tried a "**Cordon** of Concrete." It was his strongest wall yet! But, lo and behold, it failed too! That idea that had been too strong for his other walls was just too strong for a "Cordon of Concrete."

Finally, the leader decided to build the wall of the strongest material he could find. So up went his "Steel Curtain." It was constructed of the best steel money (Hueslandian tax money) could buy. But you already know the outcome. This wall failed too! You see there was an

Another time . . . Another place:
"Remember, remember always, that all of us, and you and I especially, are descended from immigrants and revolutionists."
— **Franklin D. Roosevelt**

idea stronger than steel.

In fact, the leader could have built the wall out of diamonds-the hardest thing on the planet! But it too would have failed. It would have failed because of that idea.

And what idea was so strong that walls could not stop it? Well, that was simple. It was the idea on which Hueslandia had been founded. It was ….

FREEDOM!!

Finally, it was time for a new election in Hueslandia. The citizens had grown tired of their leader's behavior. Of his lies. Of his cruelty. Of his appeal to the "lesser of their angels." And so, he was voted out of office!

The new leader soon took the oath of office. She was a person of **compassion** and of **wisdom**, and of **character**. She did not believe in open borders for Hueslandia, but instead she worked for a sane and safe immigration policy. She stopped **demonizing** the immigrants. She stopped the separation of families at the border. She developed a pathway to citizenship for the "Dreamers." She worked with all political parties to develop a new immigration policy that was fair and safe and **humane**. She worked with the leaders of the countries from which many of the immigrants had **emigrated**. She worked to end gang violence, and civil war, and religious persecution in those nations. She helped them to develop their economies and to expand their peoples' freedoms so that the

reasons for coming to Hueslandia were

reduced. She made things better for all.

And as for the Hueslandians themselves.

The better angels of their nature had won.

Many of them began to realize that they all

were immigrants, in some way, to

Hueslandia. And they also began to realize

it didn't matter what was the hue of the

person. Their skin color didn't matter. Their

religion didn't matter.

What mattered was that they were

committed to the **ideals** of Hueslandia.

Committed to the freedoms that

Hueslandians enjoyed. That they not only

desired those same freedoms—but would

defend and protect them as well.

And when that happened Hueslandia

truly became a nation of many hues.

Afterword

Once again . . . in a different time and at a different place:

Of the fifty-six signers of The Declaration of Independence, forty-nine were born in what would become The United States of America. Seven were not. Those seven were, in effect, immigrants.

New York signer **Francis Lewis** born in Llandaff, Wales in 1713.

Pennsylvania signer **James Wilson** born in Carskerdo, Scotland in 1742.

Pennsylvania signer **Robert Morris** born in Lancashire, England in 1734.

Pennsylvania signer **James Smith** born in Ireland in 1719.

Pennsylvania signer **George Taylor** born in Ireland in 1716.

Georgia signer **Button Gwinnett** born in Gloucester, England in 1735.

New Hampshire signer **Matthew Thornton** born in Ireland in 1714.

VOCABULARY BUILDER: GLOSSARY OF KEY TERMS

Allies- a state formally cooperating with another for a military or other purpose.

Amnesty- an official pardon for people who have been convicted of political offenses.

Assimilation- the absorption and integration of people, ideas, or culture into a wider society or culture.

Asylum- the protection granted by a nation to someone who has left their native country as a political refugee.

Character- the mental and moral qualities distinctive to an individual.

Compassion- sympathetic pity and concern for the sufferings or misfortunes of others.

Cordon- prevent access to or from an area or building by surrounding it with police or other guards.

Dehumanizing- depriving a person or group of positive human qualities.

Demonizing- portray as wicked and threatening.

Deportation- the action of deporting a foreigner from a country; to expel (a foreigner) from a country, typically on the grounds of illegal status or for having committed a crime.

Discrimination- the unjust or prejudicial treatment of different
categories of people or things, especially on
the grounds of race, age, or sex.

Disheartening- causing someone to lose determination or
confidence; discouraging or dispiriting.

Divisive- tending to cause disagreement or hostility between
people.

Emigrated- to leave one's own country to settle permanently in
another

Especially- used to single out one person, thing, or situation over
all others

Formidable- inspiring fear or respect through being impressively
large, powerful, intense, or capable.

Freedom- the condition of not being controlled by another nation
or political power; political independence.

Hues- colors or shades.

Humane- having or showing compassion or benevolence.

Ideal- standard of perfection; a principle to be aimed at.

Incentive- a thing that motivates or encourages one to do
something.

Inquisitor- a person making an inquiry, especially one seen to be
excessively harsh or searching.

Melting pot- a place where a variety of races, cultures, or
        individuals assimilate into a cohesive whole.

Non-violence- abstention from violence as a matter of principle;
        nonviolent demonstrations for the purpose of
        securing political ends.

Ostracism- exclusion from a society or group.

Perilous- full of danger or risk.

Persecution- hostility and ill-treatment, especially because of race
        or political or religious beliefs.

Persistent- continuing firmly or obstinately in a course of action in
        spite of difficulty or opposition.

Poverty- the state of one who lacks a usual or socially acceptable
        amount of money or material possessions; the state or
        condition of having little or no money, goods, or means
        of support; condition of being poor.

Prosperity- successful in material terms; flourishing financially;
        bringing wealth and success.

Quota- a fixed minimum or maximum number of a particular
        group of people allowed to do something, such as
        immigrants to enter a country.

Racism- prejudice or discrimination directed against
        a person or people based on their membership in a
        racial or ethnic group, typically one that is a
        minority or marginalized; the belief that different races
        possess distinct characteristics, abilities, or qualities,
        especially to distinguish them as inferior or superior

to one another.

Siege- to assail or assault; a series of illnesses, troubles, or annoyances besetting a person or group.

Stereotypes- a widely held but fixed and oversimplified image or idea of a particular type of person or thing.

Undocumented- lacking documents required for legal immigration or residence.

Vicious- deliberately cruel or violent; immoral.

Vile- extremely unpleasant; morally bad; wicked.

Wisdom- the soundness of an action or decision regarding the application of experience, knowledge, and good judgment.

Work ethic- the principle that hard work is virtuous or worthy of reward.

LIST OF SOURCES FOR DEFINITIONS

Merriam-Webster: available at https://www.merriam-webster.com/dictionary.

Oxford Dictionaries: available at https://www.oxfordlearnersdictionaries.com.

The Free Dictionary: available at https://www.thefreedictionary.com.

ACTIVITIES FOR YOUNGER READERS

On the next few pages view activities designed for younger readers.

Activity#1: On the following page use colored pencils or crayons to color this picture of a Hueslandian. Make him any hue you like. People of all hues are welcome in Hueslandia.

Activity #2-Crossword Puzzle

Hueslandia

Name:_____

Complete the crossword puzzle below with key vocabulary from the story.

Created using the Crossword Maker on TheTeachersCorner.net

Across

3. a place where a variety of races, cultures, or individuals assimilate into a cohesive whole.

8. sympathetic pity and concern for the sufferings or misfortunes of others

12. a thing that motivates or encourages one to do something

13. causing someone to lose determination or confidence; discouraging or dispiriting

15. full of danger or risk

17. The condition of not being controlled by another nation or political power; political independence

19. the absorption and integration of people, ideas, or culture into a wider society or culture.

22. having or showing compassion or benevolence

23. to assail or assault; a series of illnesses, troubles, or annoyances besetting a person or gro

24. the protection granted by a nation to someone who has left their native country as a political refugee.

Down

1. lacking documents required for legal immigration or residence

2. a widely held but fixed and oversimplified image or idea of a particular type of person or thing.

4. a color or shade

5. the mental and moral qualities distinctive to an individual

6. the unjust or prejudicial treatment of different categories of people or things

7. condition of being poor

9. a person making an inquiry, especially one seen to be excessively harsh or searching

10. to expel (a foreigner) from a country, typically on the grounds of illegal status

11. tending to cause disagreement or hostility between people

14. prevent access to or from an area or building by surrounding it with police or other guards.

16. an official pardon for people who have been convicted of political offenses

18. prejudice, discrimination, or antagonism directed against a person or people

20. standard of perfection; a principle to be aimed at.

21. a fixed minimum or maximum number of a particular group of people allowed to do something

Activity #3-Research

Go to your local library or use the Internet to find out more about the topics listed below:

1. The Pilgrims, Puritans, and Quakers

2. The Irish Potato Famine

3. Abraham Lincoln and the Emancipation Proclamation

4. Ellis Island

5. The National Origins Act

6. Lyndon Johnson and the Great Society

7. Martin Luther King, Jr.

8. The Berlin Wall

9. The Great Wall of China

10. Cesar Chavez and the United Farm Workers

Activity #4-Word Search

Name: _____

Hueslandia

Directions: Find the words from the list below in the word search puzzle. Words may be forwards, backwards, up and down, or diagonal.

```
Q  O  J  T  I  Y  U  L  J  X  J  V  H  H  N  F  H  P  N  W  X  W  A  W  F
E  G  Y  H  M  G  A  C  T  Z  O  Z  E  V  Q  E  T  J  V  Y  G  U  G  M  V
M  V  N  O  U  E  Q  O  W  E  R  K  X  M  X  I  W  R  H  O  E  W  K  V  D
L  V  N  K  L  M  K  X  C  Q  M  W  O  H  J  R  C  B  Q  Y  D  B  O  S  G
O  G  O  N  Y  F  O  C  W  O  M  G  G  S  P  A  H  I  G  Y  J  G  F  E  X
M  T  Y  N  Q  D  D  L  U  H  P  B  F  Y  T  X  U  J  O  U  N  K  E  W  A
B  T  G  T  V  O  Z  E  D  K  K  G  Y  R  J  R  M  F  M  B  P  A  Y  L  J
D  A  F  M  O  Y  T  I  G  K  T  X  J  I  H  O  A  I  O  B  I  X  L  F  O
H  B  Z  N  B  E  O  B  G  G  B  S  E  Y  T  P  N  C  Y  X  S  I  E  G  E
R  N  O  P  O  L  Z  B  X  B  O  U  B  F  T  E  E  D  I  C  E  N  L  C  A
N  P  Q  N  E  J  M  L  W  U  Z  W  I  G  K  T  W  J  V  S  L  Q  Y  A  A
A  K  O  H  R  X  J  X  K  S  T  C  Y  N  D  Z  R  E  A  M  M  T  C  W  Q
G  X  T  Q  G  K  O  J  W  M  L  A  K  A  T  O  U  Q  L  O  R  T  Y  W  J
H  Y  M  A  I  U  Z  W  X  C  Y  C  F  H  K  V  S  Z  P  E  I  T  M  T  E
P  C  A  F  H  L  J  M  I  D  F  O  K  H  E  J  I  A  V  F  Z  C  J  T  Q
Y  J  M  L  C  Y  W  W  V  I  E  B  X  H  M  G  T  O  H  Z  L  G  N  W  Z
G  I  U  U  K  I  Q  L  M  W  Y  A  Y  J  R  D  P  H  X  T  L  A  S  U  C
C  I  Z  K  S  A  G  Z  X  V  Z  A  A  M  V  Y  C  I  P  D  N  X  S  M  H
M  C  S  D  G  A  T  I  U  G  C  Q  M  A  J  E  B  E  E  R  M  J  Q  I  T
O  X  O  V  G  S  B  G  P  N  I  W  J  M  M  K  V  B  D  Y  G  C  A  H  V
S  M  A  M  N  E  S  T  Y  J  T  B  Y  Q  H  X  G  I  I  Y  W  P  A  Y  C
C  I  Y  R  E  D  A  I  N  C  E  N  T  I  V  E  O  S  L  A  E  D  I  E  N
S  W  B  H  H  R  C  N  O  I  O  M  J  N  W  P  T  B  Y  E  O  O  S  R  I
V  C  R  Q  Z  N  O  D  R  O  C  D  R  V  X  Y  M  A  F  B  R  A  F  I  U
Y  W  M  L  W  V  D  Y  J  R  W  A  W  V  S  V  Q  F  G  T  V  T  L  Q  C
```

allies	amnesty	cordon
humane	ideals	incentive
ostracism	poverty	quota
siege	vile	wisdom

ACTIVITY #5-MAZE CRAZE

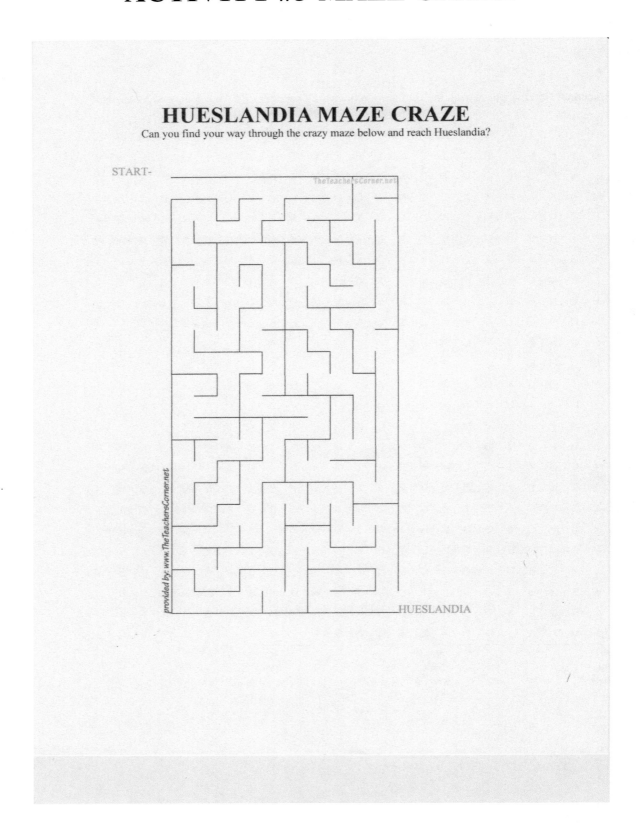

HUESLANDIA MAZE CRAZE
Can you find your way through the crazy maze below and reach Hueslandia?

SOLUTIONS

On the following pages are the answer keys to the various puzzle activities included in this book.

Name:_____

Hueslandia

Complete the crossword puzzle below with key vocabulary from the story.

Created using the Crossword Maker on TheTeachersCorner.net

Across

3. a place where a variety of races, cultures, or individuals assimilate into a cohesive whole. (**melting-pot**)
8. sympathetic pity and concern for the sufferings or misfortunes of others (**compassion**)
12. a thing that motivates or encourages one to do something (**incentive**)
13. causing someone to lose determination or confidence; discouraging or dispiriting (**disheartening**)
15. full of danger or risk (**perilous**)
17. The condition of not being controlled by another nation or political power; political independence (**freedom**)
19. the absorption and integration of people, ideas, or culture into a wider society or culture. (**assimilation**)
22. having or showing compassion or benevolence (**humane**)
23. to assail or assault; a series of illnesses, troubles, or annoyances besetting a person or gro (**siege**)
24. the protection granted by a nation to someone who has left their native country as a political refugee. (**asylum**)

Down

1. lacking documents required for legal immigration or residence (**undocumented**)
2. a widely held but fixed and oversimplified image or idea of a particular type of person or thing. (**sterotypes**)
4. a color or shade (**hues**)
5. the mental and moral qualities distinctive to an individual (**character**)
6. the unjust or prejudicial treatment of different categories of people or things (**discrimination**)
7. condition of being poor (**poverty**)
9. a person making an inquiry, especially one seen to be excessively harsh or searching (**inquistors**)
10. to expel (a foreigner) from a country, typically on the grounds of illegal status (**deportation**)
11. tending to cause disagreement or hostility between people (**divisive**)
14. prevent access to or from an area or building by surrounding it with police or other guards. (**cordon**)
16. an official pardon for people who have been convicted of political offenses (**amnesty**)
18. prejudice, discrimination, or antagonism directed against a person or people (**racism**)
20. standard of perfection; a principle to be aimed at. (**ideals**)
21. a fixed minimum or maximum number of a particular group of people allowed to do something (**quota**)

Hueslandia

Directions: Find the words from the list below in the word search puzzle. Words may be forwards, backwards, up and down, or diagonal.

```
Q  O  J  T  I  Y  U  L  J  X  J  V  H  H  N  F  H  P  N  W  X  W  A  W  F
E  G  Y  H  M  G  A  C  T  Z  O  Z  E  V  Q  E  T  J  V  Y  G  U  G  M  V
M  V  N  O  U  E  Q  O  W  E  R  K  X  M  X  I  W  R  H  O  E  W  K  V  D
L  V  N  K  L  M  K  X  C  Q  M  W  O  H  J  R  C  B  Q  Y  D  B  O  S  G
O  G  O  N  Y  F  O  C  W  O  M  G  G  S  P  A  H  I  G  Y  J  G  F  E  X
M  T  Y  N  Q  D  D  L  U  H  P  B  F  Y  T  X  U  J  O  U  N  K  E  W  A
B  T  G  T  V  O  Z  E  D  K  K  G  Y  R  J  R  M  F  M  B  P  A  Y  L  J
D  A  F  M  O  Y  T  I  G  K  T  X  J  I  H  O  A  I  O  B  I  X  L  F  L
H  B  Z  N  B  E  O  B  G  G  B  S  E  Y  T  P  N  C  Y  X  S  I  E  G  E
R  N  O  P  O  L  Z  B  X  B  O  U  B  F  T  E  E  D  I  C  E  N  L  C  A
N  P  Q  N  E  J  M  L  W  U  Z  W  I  G  K  T  W  J  V  S  L  Q  Y  A  A
A  K  O  H  R  X  J  X  K  S  T  C  Y  N  D  Z  R  E  A  M  M  T  C  W  Q
G  X  T  Q  G  K  O  J  W  M  L  A  K  A  T  O  U  Q  L  O  R  T  Y  W  J
H  Y  M  A  I  U  Z  W  X  C  Y  C  F  H  K  V  S  Z  P  E  I  T  M  T  E
P  C  A  F  H  L  J  M  I  D  F  O  K  H  E  J  I  A  V  F  Z  C  J  T  Q
Y  J  M  L  C  Y  W  W  V  I  E  B  X  H  M  G  T  O  H  Z  L  G  N  W  Z
G  I  U  U  K  I  Q  L  M  W  Y  A  Y  J  R  D  P  H  X  T  L  A  S  U  C
C  I  Z  K  S  A  G  Z  X  V  Z  A  A  M  V  Y  C  I  P  D  N  X  S  M  H
M  C  S  D  G  A  T  I  U  G  C  Q  M  A  J  E  B  E  E  R  M  J  Q  I  T
O  X  O  V  G  S  B  G  P  N  I  W  J  M  M  K  V  B  D  Y  G  C  A  H  V
S  M  A  M  N  E  S  T  Y  J  T  B  Y  Q  H  X  G  I  I  Y  W  P  A  Y  C
C  I  Y  R  E  D  A  I  N  C  E  N  T  I  V  E  O  S  L  A  F  D  I  E  N
S  W  B  H  H  R  C  N  O  I  O  M  J  N  W  P  T  B  Y  E  O  O  S  R  I
V  C  R  Q  Z  N  O  D  R  O  C  D  R  V  X  Y  M  A  F  B  R  A  F  I  U
Y  W  M  L  W  V  D  Y  J  R  W  A  W  V  S  V  Q  F  G  T  V  T  L  Q  C
```

allies	amnesty	cordon
humane	ideals	incentive
ostracism	poverty	quota
siege	vile	wisdom

HUESLANDIA MAZE CRAZE

Can you find your way through the crazy maze below and reach Hueslandia?

START-

HUESLANDIA

Acknowledgements

I would like to express my gratitude to Carissa McDonald for the wonderful and creative illustrations she developed for this book. Her imaginative and colorful artwork adds immeasurably to the book's value and message.

I would also like to recognize a very special website-The TeacherCorners.net. This website was utilized for the development of the puzzle and maze activities that supplement this work. This site is a wonderful source for teachers, educators, and parents. It is easy to use and offers a myriad of activities and lesson plans for enhancing educational experiences both in and out of the classroom.

Finally, I would like to thank my wife, Lori, for her love and encouragement. She has always been a rock of support for whatever endeavors I have chosen to pursue in our forty-plus years of marriage.

About the author: Michael Murphy is a retired educator from Missouri who taught for over twenty-five years in Missouri's public schools and colleges. He holds a Bachelor of Arts degree in history and political science from Murray State University and a Master of Social Science in History and Sociology from the University of Mississippi. He is the author of *Elsie's Story: This Story Has No Hero* and *Lucky 13: Mort Cooper and the Jinx That Led to a MVP Season*. His work has also appeared in *Instructor, Good Old Days Magazine, Poet Forum,* and the *Annual Conference of the Missouri National Guard Association Guidebook.*

About the illustrator: Carissa McDonald is a photographer, artist, and illustrator who is also from Missouri. She holds a Bachelor's degree in Photography from Southeast Missouri State University where she also studied art. She illustrated *Elsie's Story: This Story Has No Hero* and provided several illustrations for *Lucky 13: Mort Cooper and the Jinx That Led to a MVP Season.* Her photographic and artistic portfolio can be viewed at carissamcd.wixsite.com/photography.